Frog Crush
Colouring Book

Part of
The Crush Series

This book belongs to:

....

The Crush Hippo

The Crush Fish

The Crush Frog

The Crush Fly

The Crush Crocodile

The
Crush
Frog

The
Crush
Frog

The
Crush
Fish

The
Crush
Fish

The
Crush
Croc

The
Crush
Hippo

"I am a hippo, a great grey hippo, waddling along...
I am a hippo, a great big hippo, singing a song!"

The Crush Hippo

Do you know that a male hippo
can grow up to 3.5 m long, 1.5 m tall
and it can weigh up to 3.2 tonnes?

This is as much as 3 small cars!

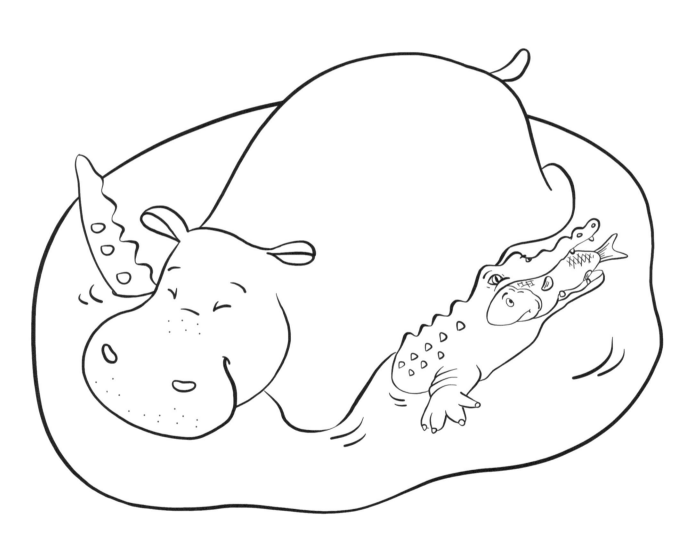

The
Crush
World

... and frogs like to eat flies.

Fish like to eat frogs ...

Did you know?

The Crush Maze

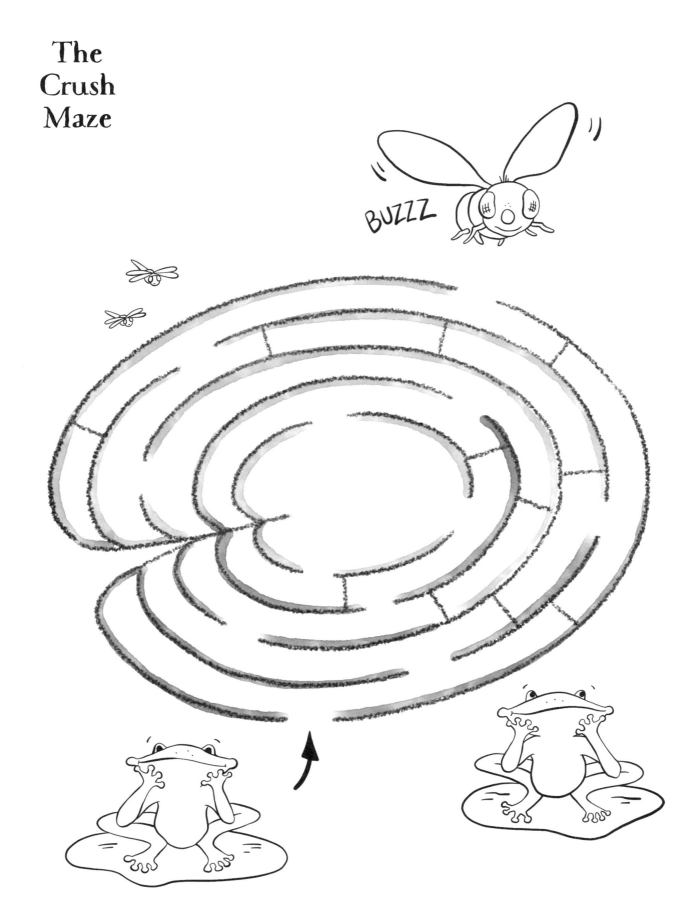

Will you help the frog find his way to the fly?

Can you draw
nice wings for the fly?

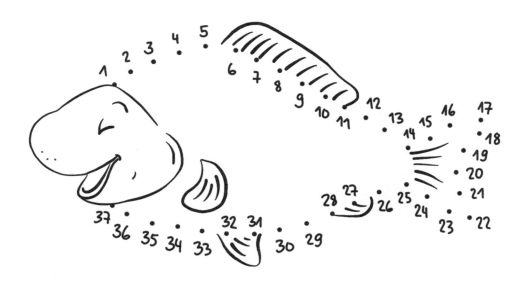

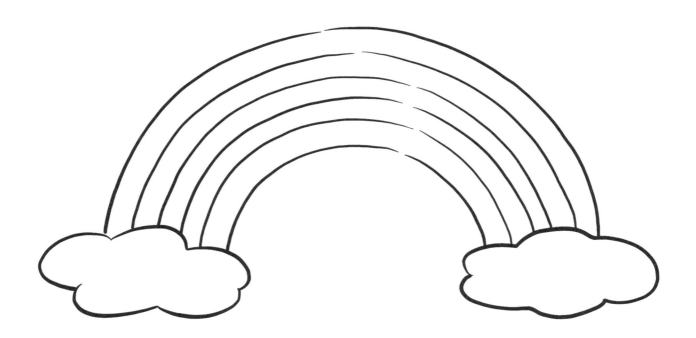

Draw your favorite animal
into our shop window,
so that the Crush Hippo knows what you like!

Books in The Crush Series

New releases to come:
✯ Crab Crush, Elephant Crush ✯

Colouring Books

Puzzles

Treat your kids to something fun,
a Hippo T-shirt for in the sun.
Or maybe a Frog, or a Crocodile,
so browse our shop for fun and style.

Quiz Cards

T-shirts

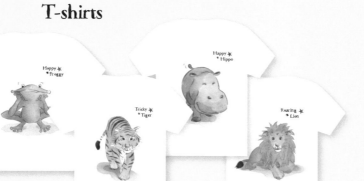